Porpoise or Dolphin

Which Is Which?

By Tamra B. Orr

21st Century Junior Library

Published in the United States of America by
Cherry Lake Publishing
Ann Arbor, Michigan
www.cherrylakepublishing.com

Reading Adviser: Marla Conn, MS, Ed., Literacy specialist, Read-Ability, Inc.
Content Adviser: Susan Heinrichs Gray

Photo Credits: ©BrendanHunter/iStock, cover (left); ©Willyam Bradberry/Shutterstock, cover (right); ©Ruth Hartnup/flickr, 4; ©Normana Karia/Shutterstock, 6; ©Elise V/Shutterstock, 8; ©jasperdenboer_photography/Shutterstock, 10; ©jivz/iStock, 12; ©vkilikov/Shutterstock, 14; ©Ecomare/Salko de Wolf/Wikimedia/Creative Commons Attribution-Share Alike 4.0 International, 16, 20; ©Alessandro De Maddalena/Shutterstock, 18

Library of Congress Cataloging-in-Publication Data

Names: Orr, Tamra, author.
Title: Porpoise or dolphin / Tamra B. Orr.
Description: Ann Arbor : Cherry Lake Publishing, [2019] | Series: Which is which? | Includes bibliographical references and index. | Audience: K to Grade 3.
Identifiers: LCCN 2019005988 | ISBN 9781534147362 (hardcover) | ISBN 9781534150225 (paperback) | ISBN 9781534148796 (pdf) | ISBN 9781534151659 (hosted ebook)
Subjects: LCSH: Porpoises—Juvenile literature. | Dolphins—Juvenile literature.
Classification: LCC QL737.C434 O77 2019 | DDC 599.53—dc23
LC record available at https://lccn.loc.gov/2019005988

Cherry Lake Publishing would like to acknowledge the work of the Partnership for 21st Century Skills. Please visit *www.p21.org* for more information.

Printed in the United States of America
Corporate Graphics

CONTENTS

Some porpoises can swim over 30 miles (48 kilometers) per hour in order to escape danger.

Fins in the Water

See that fin sticking out of the water? Does it belong to a dolphin or a porpoise? Look closely. Can you spot the differences? Can you tell which is which? It can be hard to tell since the two **mammals** are very **similar**. The **dorsal** fin, which is the fin that sticks out of the water, is one of the best clues. If it's shaped like a triangle, it belongs to a porpoise. If it is curved, the creature is a dolphin.

Porpoises and dolphins are different types of **cetaceans**. But they have a lot in common.

Pectoral fins are also called flippers.

Both are mammals, not fish. They give birth to live young and **nurse** them. They have lungs, not gills. This means they breathe air. They have three kinds of fins. The dorsal fin helps direct where these animals swim. The **pectoral** fins have bones in them much like the bones in human hands and arms. They are used for stopping and steering in water. The tail fins are called flukes. These don't have any bones. They help these sea creatures race through the water.

Look!

Did you know that the flippers of a dolphin and porpoise are similar to human hands? Using the internet or your library, study the bones of these two animals. Can you see how they are alike?

Despite being able to dive over 650 feet (198 meters) deep, porpoises like to find their food in shallow water by the coast.

Teeth and Talking

A closer look at dolphins and porpoises shows other differences. Dolphins have a long body, big mouth, and a long, beak-like nose. They commonly grow to 10 feet (3 meters) long. But they can be even longer! The longest type of dolphin is more than 30 feet (9 m) long.

Porpoises have smaller bodies and mouths. Their nose looks squashed. They

Dolphins make more communicative noise than porpoises. They make whistling sounds using their blowhole.

usually do not grow past 7 feet (2 m) long. Looking inside the mammals' mouths brings another important clue. Porpoises have spade or shovel-shaped teeth. Dolphins have cone-shaped teeth.

There is another difference between dolphins and porpoises. You would hear it if you could swim underwater with them. Porpoises seem quiet. They make sounds too high for human ears to hear. Dolphins are noisy. They whistle, click, and chirp. Both mammals use their **blowholes** to make their different sounds.

Porpoises have spatula-shaped teeth. Dolphins have pointy teeth. Pictured is a shy porpoise with its mouth closed.

Animals "talk" to each other through these sounds. They also use them as part of **echolocation**. This is used to find food and escape from **predators**. It also helps them find their way around in the dark water. Both mammals use a special feature in their foreheads called a melon. It makes and sends out sound waves. These waves bounce off objects and back to the mammals' ears. This allows them to "see" with sound.

Ask Questions!

What other types of creatures use echolocation? What do they use it for? Is it different from how dolphins and porpoises use it?

Young dolphins tend to stick with their mom for 3 to 8 years.

Pods and Play

If you spot a fin in the water, chances are you are seeing a dolphin. Why? First, porpoises are shy and cautious around humans, but dolphins are not. Dolphins are known for swimming alongside swimmers and boats. They have even helped drowning people reach safety. Stories from ancient times even tell about the friendships between humans and dolphins. Second, porpoises tend to live in small **pods** of two to four.

Dolphins are far more social than porpoises. Porpoises tend to keep their group small and avoid boats and humans.

But dolphins live in pods of 10 to 20. "Super pods" may have as many as 1,000.

Have you ever seen a mammal leap fully out of the water? You're most likely witnessing a dolphin. They often leap in the air for fun! Porpoises almost never do this. Dolphins also live longer than porpoises. Porpoises rarely live longer than 20 years. Dolphins commonly live 50 years or more.

Make a Guess!

The killer whale is actually a type of dolphin. Look up images of the whale. How is it like and unlike other dolphins? How did it earn the name "killer" whale?

We don't have to think about breathing, but dolphins and porpoises do. They have to decide when to surface the water and take a deep breath.

Brainy Mammals

Dolphins and porpoises are also smart! They are often called the most **intelligent** creatures in the world, next to humans.

Porpoises are quite clever. They can be taught to do simple tricks and tasks by a trainer. However, dolphins take first prize when it comes to intelligence. They can do difficult tricks and moves on command. They are often seen in marine parks entertaining crowds with their feats. Dolphins can look in the mirror and recognize themselves. Dolphins also have

Scientists claim that dolphins and porpoises are so intelligent that they can recognize themselves in the mirror, like humans!

their own special whistle, similar to having a name. Dolphins in a pod sometimes whistle their own names. This helps other dolphins know who's there. Dolphins can even imitate each other's special whistle. They do this to check up on each other.

Dolphins and porpoises are some of the world's most amazing creatures. They are very much alike in many ways. Each is special, though, and worth getting to know better.

Think!

Dolphins and porpoises are protected **species**. That means hunting them is illegal. Doing so can result in anything from large fines to time in jail. What other animals are on the protected list? What is required for them to be put on this list?

GLOSSARY

blowholes (BLOH-hohlz) holes on the top of the heads of porpoises, dolphins, or whales through which they breathe

cetaceans (sih-TAY-shuhnz) marine mammals that usually have a hairless body, paddle-shaped fins toward the front, and a flat tail

dorsal (DOR-suhl) on or toward the back of an animal

echolocation (ek-oh-loh-KAY-shuhn) using sound waves in order to see, find their way, and hunt

intelligent (in-TEL-ih-juhnt) quick to understand, think, and learn

mammals (MAM-uhlz) animals that feed milk to their young and usually have hair or fur covering most of their body

nurse (NURS) produce milk to feed a baby

pectoral (PEK-tor-uhl) on or toward the chest of an animal

pods (PAHDZ) a group of dolphins, porpoises, or other sea animals

predators (PRED-uh-turz) animals that live by hunting other animals for food

similar (SIM-uh-lur) nearly but not exactly alike

species (SPEE-sheez) a group of animals that are similar and can produce young animals

FIND OUT MORE

BOOKS

Hoyt, Erich. *Encyclopedia of Whales, Dolphins, and Porpoises.* Richmond Hill, ON: Firefly Books, 2017.

Morgan, Sally. *Dolphins and Porpoises.* Mankato, MN: QEB Publishing, 2014.

Pringle, Laurence. *Dolphins! Strange and Wonderful.* Honesdale, PA: Boyds Mills Press, 2019.

Ryndak, Rob. *Dolphin or Porpoise?* New York, NY: Gareth Stevens, 2016.

Shepherd, Jodie. *Porpoises.* New York, NY: Children's Press, 2018.

WEBSITES

Science Trends—Porpoise vs Dolphin: The Difference
https://sciencetrends.com/comparing-dolphins-vs-porpoises-how-to-easily-tell-them-apart
Discover more fascinating facts about porpoises and dolphins.

YouTube—Dolphins vs Porpoises
https://www.youtube.com/watch?v=gwdovKB_2xw
Watch an informative video about the differences and similarities between these two amazing animals.

INDEX

ABOUT THE AUTHOR

Tamra Orr is the author of hundreds of books for readers of all ages. She graduated from Ball State University, but moved with her husband and four children to Oregon in 2001. She is a full-time author, and when she isn't researching and writing, she writes letters to friends all over the world. Orr enjoys life in the big city of Portland, and has taken many trips to nearby Seattle to visit the aquarium and the dolphins and porpoises she sees there.

21st Century **Junior** Library

The 21st Century Junior Library introduces young readers to important core content. Simple activities encourage students to **Look**, **Think**, **Make a Guess**, **Ask Questions**, and **Create**. The combination of reading and inquiring helps them develop the skills needed to master content and learn and succeed in the 21st century.

Read all of these 21st Century Junior Library titles to learn about **Which Is Which?**:

Aardvark or Anteater
Alpaca or Llama
Butterfly or Moth
Crocodile or Alligator
Frog or Toad
Porpoise or Dolphin
Seal or Sea Lion
Wasp or Bee

GR: N

ISBN-13: 978-1534150225

9 781534 150225

CHERRY LAKE Publishing

www.cherrylakepublishing.com

my itty-bitty bio

Gwen Frostic